A Change of Direction

Frances Thimann

First Published in the UK in 2019 by Mantle Lane Press

ISBN 978-1-9160570-0-5

Mantle Lane Press
Springboard Centre
Mantle Lane
Coalville
LE67 3DW
www.mantlelanepress.co.uk
www.mantlearts.org.uk

Printed and bound in the UK by
Imprint Digital, Upton Pyne, Exeter, EX5 5HY

Cover illustration by Nina Goodyer
ninagoodyer.co.uk

Contents

The Indus Seals

My boy Will come back last month.

I went up on the train to see him in the hospital, big new place in Birmingham. Six weeks before he gets home, they said. And then he'll have to take it quiet, not do too much. Not for a while.

I say my boy but that don't seem right no more. It's Will's name on the end of the bed, but it's not my lad lying there, like. Someone different, they got Will's name up by mistake.

I won't say it wasn't a shock, like, seeing him that first time.

All he said was, "Thanks for coming, Dad," when I got there, and then he didn't say much else the rest of the time. I sat with him, just quiet. Once, he says, "Pass me the water, would you, Dad?" and I passed him the glass so he could reach it. I put his hand round it, watched him while he drank a bit. I had to go soon after that because of the doctor wanting to see him.

We called him Will, his mum and me, after Prince William. We reckoned he was better-looking though, growing up, everyone thought that, it wasn't just we was his mum and dad.

Derek at the factory, does nights, he lost his brother, only been married three years. There's a good few of us at work got family affected, one way or another. A lot of the lads round here go in the Army, not much for the youngsters to do these days, things closing down all over.

They say next year the troops'll be coming home. I've not followed it all, what's gone on, why they went out there to start with, they was always saying something new. But there's plenty said different, our Leanne for one.

"How's our Leanne?" Will says that second time I'm up there. "How's she getting on with them clever types at college?" I was sitting quiet, like, in his room, neither of us talking much. Nice room.

He was a lovely boy – fair hair, blond almost, same as his mum, brown eyes. She spoilt him terrible. We called him Will after the Prince.

My girl Leanne, she's the one with the brains, just started at uni. Studying History, *reading* History she's pleased to call it. So there's Will out there fighting, part of the history, like, and our Leanne studying up about it all. They was always scrapping as kids, she was out to prove she could do what her older brother did and more, we couldn't ever stop them, but now Will's… now things is the way they are, Leanne's quite different with him, can't do enough, like she's making up for all the wars they had. She didn't go in the Army same as him though, not her style.

She visits him regular. Very upset she was, that first time.

I don't recall much history from school. Churchill and the War, we thought that was the best part, the Tudors and Stuarts didn't mean a lot to us lads back then. "You ought to know more about it, Dad, fix up an evening class or something," Leanne says, serious, like, the way she is, but I'd not fit in. All them ladies. Not my style.

I used to like a good book, anything with a bit of a mystery I could work out, who-dunnits and such. But I can't get into them these days, keep losing track, not sleeping too well neither. No good getting into bed and lying there staring at the ceiling. I picked up one of Leanne's she'd left lying about, she said it was on the radio. It's a great thick one, but the chapters is quite short.

"I think you'd enjoy it, Dad," she tells me, "it's about things people have made, the same as you did, ordinary people quite often." There's photographs and pictures, maps and such all through it. Like I said, she's the brains of the family. Not much of a looker, skinny little thing, not like her brother, but always top of her class at school.

It was the pictures got me interested. When the kids was small I took to making toys for them, carving bits of wood I got from work, models for Will, helping him put them together, making 'em go. Bits and pieces for the train set and the dolls' house and such. Knocked up a rabbit hutch for the neighbours' lot. Always been good with my hands. Making things, it was a hobby, like, and they went down a treat with all the kids. Don't know where they've finished up now, them bits of things I made.

My Tess was always telling me to get rid of the dust and mess, clear it all up. But she was pleased with them too, her face was a picture. "You've got hidden talents, George," she says.

In this book, the pictures was of carvings, pots, all sorts, chessmen, things people made, just ordinary things sometimes, but they was important, at least that's what they think these days. *A History of the World in 100 Objects* it's called. I says to Leanne there must be more than a hundred objects in the history of the world, there's a good few lying around in your room, I says, sharp like, but "It's about what they mean in terms of human progress, Dad," she tells me. Made me think about Will, still up there in the hospital.

Looking through the pictures is a treat. *Swimming Reindeer* – lovely bit of carving, that – *Jade Dragon Cup*, *Double-headed Serpent*. Makes you want to read up about them all. So now I'm reading History too, like.

I picked out this chapter, *Indus Seal*, about some things they found up in India and Pakistan, near where Will was fighting, that's why it caught my eye. I looked it up on the map. Me and the wife was planning a holiday in India a few years back, palaces and forts, the Taj Mahal, elephants and such. Not my style, but Tess liked all that kind of thing.

That would've been our twentieth. Tess wanted something special, said she always fancied a trip to India. Like a kid herself, sometimes, she was. "*Peacocks and Palaces*, George," she reads out, looking through the booklet. "That's the one for us. We're going to see the world, George," she tells me. Her face was a picture.

Twenty-five it would've been, next month. Sweet girl she was, my Tess, when I fell for her, brown eyes same as Will, fair hair, just the same. Took to putting streaks in it later, different colour each week.

I won't say it wasn't a shock, like, when she passed away so sudden. Very sudden, it all was.

"You take care of the kids, George," she says, last thing.

Now Will's back home, the nights is the worst. He wakes up sweating and screaming, shaking all over. Next day he's lying there staring at the ceiling. That first night I heard all the noise and I went in his room, saw what was happening. I tried to hold him quiet, calm him down, put my arms round him, they didn't go all round, he's a good bit bigger than me, been bigger since he was fourteen. I got him better after a bit, fumbling about, awkward, like, talking to him, anything I could think of: football results, next door's goings on, anything. Just holding him, in the dark, it was something deep, like, just a boy and his dad, might've been any time, any place in the world. I'd not done nothing like that since he was a lad and he fell off his bike, hurt his knees. Always left that side of things to the wife.

"Thanks Dad," he says, a bit later. Just that. "Thanks, Dad. OK now."

This chapter in the book was about the ruins they found up there, towns, big ones, no-one knew about them for thousands of years till Victorian times and there's a lot they still don't know, they've not found much written down. But they never discovered no fortifications, nothing military, like, and the houses was all the same, not great villas for the rich and hovels for the poor. It was planned out, proper plumbing and such. The seals was used in trade with the other countries around, so they knew how to do all right without the fighting. Working things out, democratic, like, not going to war.

Another night I go in his room, the light's on, he's still sitting in his chair, two in the morning. "I don't want to go to sleep, Dad," he says, "I don't want them bad dreams again."

Twenty-one last year, he was. They patched him up in the hospital, but there's not a lot of assistance with the rest of it now he's back home. He'll not see the doctor. "I've seen enough of them doctors," he tells me. "Dish out a lot of pills." So it's down to me to see him through, there isn't anyone else going to. It's what my Tess would have wanted.

No-one knows how it was there back in them days – there's not much written down. It's mostly just the seals they've found, for trading, quite small, with the strange animals carved on. There's one like a unicorn, and there's an elephant; and the marks, different shapes, no-one knows what they are, letters or signs, if they're a real language or not. They've been trying to work it out for years, the experts, they're still working at it.

If they could find out what them signs mean, they could find out how they managed it, how they could live together without the fighting, peaceful, like. It might change a lot of things if they could find that out.

Looking round here, I can't see any objects which might change the world. That donkey on the mantelpiece, with the hat, *Greetings From The Canaries* it says on it, neighbours brought it back last year, people might puzzle over that one day. I got rid of most of the bits and pieces when Tess passed away, they was only a reminder, never felt much like replacing them, clutter the place up. Maybe that's not the right way to think. Maybe things – objects – is important after all.

Him and Josie, his girlfriend, they was planning on getting engaged, but that's not happening now, though she's not said as much. "It's not... it's not the physical things, George, it's... " She started calling me Dad one time but it's George again now. Lovely girl. Been sweethearts for years.

"I think I'd like to go out to Canada, Dad," he says one night, as if he's made a decision. "Farming. Or New Zealand. Somewhere quiet, and cold, lots of space. Mountains." But he never does anything about it.

I might go up one day to see them things in the Museum. All the objects in the book is in the British Museum in London. Take a day trip.

Derek says, "What're you planning to see then? Phantom of the Opera? Not your style I'd have thought. New lady friend?"

I says to him, "I'm going to the British Museum, look at some seals," and his face is a picture. "Don't you mean the Zoo," he says after a bit. "You want the Aquarium."

These big ideas which change the world - how did they get started, how would you know when there's one just getting started?

I read a different chapter of the book, there was another George Smith - he was an ordinary chap, not much education, but he took an interest in the old languages and such and managed to work out a piece of writing about the Flood, like the Bible story, which showed it was written a lot earlier than they thought, earlier than the Bible, which upset all the experts.

I'd not be able to do anything like that. But I'd like to have a look, just see them, so I could get an idea. That George Smith, he changed what people thought.

"You should take up the carving again, Dad," Leanne says. "They were lovely, those little things you made for us when we were kids. You never know, it might be one of your things they're arguing about in a thousand years' time."

"Objects," I says.

I might show Will how it's done, be a bit of an interest for him, like.

There's wars and fighting going on all over – Afghanistan, Africa, out in Egypt. Terrible business in Syria.

There was a lad in the news, big dark eyes, lost both his legs, and his dad holding him with his face all screwed up crying.

When it's your own lad it's different, it's not just a picture in the news.

The fighting and the killing goes round and round like a virus, there's nothing to stop it. Maybe Leanne's right, always going off on protests and marches and such. "There's war crimes going on, Dad," she says. "It's only people like us can change it all. There isn't anyone else going to."

Maybe we're going backwards these days, there's no progress to write about any more. Maybe we're destroying all the objects we could learn from, the history, like, with the fighting and the bombing.

If we could figure out them signs we could figure out how they did it, them people back then, no soldiers, no wars, thousands of miles quiet and peaceful. I reckon figuring it out'd be better than the meetings and the marching. Maybe she's got it wrong this time, our Leanne. Just this once.

The other night Will come back blind drunk, been out with his mates. I heard him swearing and shouting, crashing about, neighbours banging on the wall, and I went in his room, helped him calm down, got his boots off.

After a bit he's crying, he's curled up on the bed, all six foot of him, snuffling and wheezing like he's an old man and there isn't nothing left, end of the road.

"I'm finished, Dad," he's saying after a bit, much quieter. "All washed up."

I'm sitting there in the dark for a long time listening to him, whining and moaning, my boy Will, second time round now, and it's like it's all connected, what's happened with him, and the other lads which didn't make it, the mums and dads and sweethearts, and them old pictures and carvings, it's a mystery, and it's connected, there's one big solution to it all.

"You take care of the kids, George," she says, my Tess, last thing.

But there's more to it, being a dad, it's knowing things, history and such, finding things out. I've fixed to go up in the train to London next week, take the day off, have a look at them seals in the Museum. I'll be clearer, seeing them letters and signs, I'll be able to get things straight in my mind, like. Sort out what it all means.

The White Cat

She had to stand on tiptoe to see herself in the little bathroom mirror; even then it was only her head and shoulders that were visible, and her breath came and went on the glass like the colour on her cheek, so that she couldn't see clearly. But the face that looked so anxiously into hers seemed prettier than ever: the soft, blue-white skin of her temples was almost transparent as if lit from within, her nose a delicate, upturned curve, her mouth like some small, ripe-red fruit, sweet and ready for eating.

As she stood before the mirror, the only one she had, Evie felt the old rodent fear, that one day she might find her face had become ugly suddenly, even disfigured - but of course, the great grey-blue eyes that regarded her were flawless now as ever, soft as smoke, changeable with the light or with her mood, almost with the air she breathed.

She wished she had a proper mirror. Sometimes she would have to look in a shop window to check her hem or the fall of her coat, and the furniture or the clothes inside became superimposed upon her as if she were a ghost there. Or she would try some dresses in a changing cubicle where she could see herself reflected more clearly, but somehow she never quite found the angle she wanted, never the whole view.

But time was running out, and still she'd not found anything she thought she could wear. The dress she'd definitely decided upon the night before, very pretty and feminine, with an old-fashioned high collar and long tight cuffs, had a button loose at the front and a small stain lower down that she noticed only when she put it on. She let it drop to the floor where it lay, twisted, as if it had suddenly become invisible to her, her feet stepped round it of themselves. She moved restlessly round the flat again as the clock began to race and leap, searching here and there amongst the shelves, opening the wardrobe, the cupboards, frowning at skeletons, dissatisfied with everything she found, panic-stricken. "Oh, this miserable place!" she whispered fiercely to herself, half-crying, and for the hundredth time. She hated the hump-backed lino and the stained furniture in every dismal shade from laurel green to chocolate brown. She hated the dark blurred patches that appeared to slither and creep across the walls when her back was turned. She wondered for the thousandth time why it was that everything was so much harder to find here, in this poky flat, than in the pretty modern house where she'd lived before, with Alan, where morning sunshine had overflowed the windows and there'd been a place for everything. And she'd been able to buy a new dress when she needed one.

She knelt before the fire in an effort to bring it back to life for it had broken down yet again. It had not been properly repaired, though the landlord had taken long enough to arrange it.

"I'll look after you, little lady," the man had muttered hoarsely, looking at every part of her with brilliant, excited eyes that seemed to leave a moist snail's trail over her body, his heavy crimson lips fallen apart. As he left he patted her bare arm lingeringly, his fingers coarse as carrots; a stale smell rose from him, and his loose belly brushed against her side like a pillow as he moved past her to the door - she knew he did it on purpose. And in the end he had let her down and the fire was still not working properly. She was always cold.

She'd been afraid of him - she was often afraid, now that she was alone.

Evie stood very still for a moment, hurried preparations all forgotten, leaning her forehead against a wall, her red-gold hair engulfing her face, eyes full of tears. These days everything she touched turned to disaster; each time it was harder to get ready, to make arrangements, to find the right clothes - sometimes she felt as if everything about her was falling apart. A few weeks ago, in a rush to prepare and hurry out early for an interview, feeling sleepy and tired still, she'd fallen and tripped over one of Chloe's toys - she scolded the child every day about leaving them out, but it made no difference - and she'd bruised her face so badly that the marks still showed, though she'd used every cream and paste she owned. The expression in the other woman's eyes shamed her still, and she'd not been offered the work, nor anything else since then. It would have been good work too, receptionist in a big firm, it might have become permanent; and now little Chloe needed so many things, and the landlord was worrying her for payment. She'd found him once, bent outside her door, his eye keyhole-shaped, and the fear that was now familiar to her flooded like sickness into her throat.

At length she shook back her hair, and her panic, as best she could. She knew, suddenly, what she would wear - she would stitch up the hem of the long dress she'd worn last Christmas, when she'd taken Chloe up to see her grandfather. They'd had a good time then. She'd been surprised, she'd only gone in desperation, not knowing what else to do, that first Christmas after Alan had left them. The old man and Chloe had got on so well, though he'd not seen her since the christening; he'd even tried to decorate the place and he'd asked Chloe to help him. It had all been a bit pathetic, but Chloe had loved it, trotting about talking to herself in the way she had, absorbed and happy as she rarely was now. For those few days, the old man's hollowed-out face, the ivory skin all fallen in amongst the bones, had filled out a little, taken on some colour. "It's that red dress of yours, love," he'd whispered. "Makes such a glow about the place."

Chloe often talked about him now and asked when they would see him again. Evie pushed the thought of him away as she'd pushed that unpleasant letter away behind the clock – it had come from his neighbour up there soon after they returned home. She hadn't known he'd been saving for a special new chair, he hadn't said anything about it to her, and she'd spent all the money he'd given her by then, there were so many things that she needed. She'd go up again soon maybe, but she couldn't think about that now.

She would quickly tack up the hem, she could sew it properly later. Alan had always loved her in red; there'd been that look in his eyes when he first saw her in the dress, that look she didn't understand but which excited her. But then there'd been so many things she hadn't understood about him...

The silky dress had a lovely double sheen, it changed colour as she moved. She hurried from room to room of the flat, a candle flickering in a draught, looking for scissors, for needle and cotton, wondering where she'd last used them. Her hair danced and burned in a tender confusion on her neck and shoulders; in the dingy room it glowed like the bright heart of fire. Her opal-white skin gleamed in the red, revealing dress. Oh, Alan had had that special way of touching her, caressing her shoulder, where there was a little strewn gold-dust of hair, with the tips of his fingers, running them gently downwards so shyly, or tracing the blue-grey veins below her throat, his dark eyes full of a silver light when he looked at her. She almost cried out, then she laughed softly and shivered: she knew she was right to wear the dress, but her arms were cold.

From the window she would look out sometimes to see the little cat next door. It was not yet full-grown, not yet a serious cat, only half-way from a kitten with the clumsiness, the delicate playfulness still of the kitten. She would watch it with Chloe, playing in the garden, chasing its tail or jumping after butterflies or birds, absorbed in itself, its fur brilliant, snowy white, its ears and nose rose pink; and Chloe's face shone and became full of laughter, almost the only time that it did so these days. But this time Evie turned away from the window - the sight of the cat upset her now. It was so small, so vulnerable; a few months ago its predecessor had been attacked by one of the big savage dogs in the neighbourhood. Nature was very cruel, she thought, cruel and unfair, it was kill or be killed. She shivered. She didn't like to think of the unpleasantness, and was afraid that Chloe might see something like that happening again. The child had been upset too and there'd been no father to console her, to kiss the tears away, to hold her tightly to his big body; no low, quiet voice to reassure. Somehow she'd always been her father's child. For days she'd been difficult.

Evie went into the tiny kitchen, made a cup of coffee under the hot tap. She started to move restlessly round the flat again, a butterfly with red-gold wings looking for the sunshine.

The bell rang. Quickly she poured the rest of the coffee down the sink, which was stained yellow-brown like a smoker's fingers, she never had time to clean it properly. Maria looked after Chloe sometimes while Evie was away. Chloe didn't like her, but she lived nearby, and didn't cost very much. Today she was early for once.

"Very cold out," Maria complained, wheezing and vast on the doorstep. The weather never suited her. Evie wondered again why it was that everyone she knew or met now had something wrong with them. She gathered up her things hastily, for she wished to avoid Maria's endless talk, her tales of misfortune, her menacing ugliness.

She went at last into Chloe's room to say goodbye. The little girl was still sleeping or pretending to sleep, her face turned away to the wall, the room still darkened. Evie knew she shouldn't really let her rest so late, but often it was easier that way: she became bad-tempered when she was woken earlier, as she became bad-tempered when taken to bed. Her long, copper-dark hair was twisted like a scarf of shining silk over one shoulder. It fell almost to her waist when she stood. A slender white arm, so like her mother's, lay over the blanket, for already she was womanly and feminine as only a four-year old can be. With the other arm she held the old red-and-white checked doll that had belonged to her mother as a girl, and was now splitting at the seams, patched and patched again. She loved it and clung to it, never appearing to want any other toy. She would cradle it in her arms, singing to it tunelessly, making up her own words. Sometimes she would throw it violently across the room. She was a lonely child, easily upset, and her mother did not have the heart to take the doll away. It might not withstand the treatment for much longer, Evie thought. Perhaps it would last just until Chloe started school in the autumn.

Evie knelt suddenly, throwing her arms impulsively about the lovely, sleeping child. She kissed the luminous ivory face and forehead, the delicate veins at the temple, smoothing them with her fingers in wonder, the skin so thin there that it seemed to expose all the tender, complex workings of the little mind within. "Oh, sweetheart," she cried, full of love and pain, "I want you to have all the prettiest things in the world, a pretty room and lovely clothes... And you will soon, my darling, I promise you… I promise…".

Chloe's eyes opened for a moment. They were dark and heavy, her father's eyes; the skin beneath them was dark too, darker than the rest of her face, and her lips were full and wide and sulky. She turned away from her mother's caresses, closing her eyes again.

"Are you going out soon?"

She said such things to hurt her mother. Evie wondered sometimes if there was something wrong with the girl, she was so cold, unresponsive, almost as if she were empty, or filled only with cotton wool or some brittle and artificial substance, like the doll.

Now all the familiar fears throbbed in Evie's own heart again, and her eyes overflowed with tears she could not control. Since Alan had left them it had been like this, fits of weeping coming upon her suddenly, without reason. It was eight months now since he'd been gone, and that had been after so many bitter words between them. At first, oh, he'd adored her, always thinking of what she might like, bringing her flowers in that shy gruff way, almost as if he were angry with her or with himself. In those first years he'd often had that look in his eyes which surprised her when she caught it: a look not of happiness but of... oh, something else that she didn't understand, as if he was hurt, or was in pain in some way; often Chloe had that same strange look. He'd been quiet and thoughtful, slow to make up his mind, to become roused; she'd never really known what he was thinking, things went so deep with him: the way he looked at her, the force of his feelings when he loved her.

But gradually, he'd changed: he'd become critical of her, almost as if he didn't care for her any more. She'd been surprised and hurt by some of the things he'd said, by his anger. In the end, they'd had a terrible argument. She was still not quite sure why it had started. She'd come home late one afternoon, very tired and not feeling well; she'd been with a few old friends just enjoying herself and the time had flown by. Maria must have gone early that day, unreliable as usual: everyone she knew let her down sooner or later. Alan came into the hall then, and he became so angry when he saw her, for a minute she thought he was going to attack her. He seized the heavy clothes brush on the table there and raised it high above his head, then suddenly he dropped it with a crash, his eyes became red and bloodshot, he sat on the chair and put his head on his arms so that all she could see was his dark hair on the white collar, his long back heaving - and he wept. It had frightened and disturbed her more than his anger, thrusting up like a volcano, dry sobs rising violently from deep within his body. Then he shouted that she neglected him and spoiled the child, that she didn't look after the house, she spent too much money, oh, and a lot of other things she could hardly remember now, about her friends, the people she went with. She'd been shocked, she'd had no idea he could think or say such things. It was as if he was talking about a different person, someone she didn't recognise, it was all distorted, a distorting mirror, she wasn't like that at all. They were very different, that was the difficulty - he'd never understood her, what she wanted from life.

She'd been even more afraid of him then. She'd run out of the house with Chloe, stayed with her sister until she thought the trouble might have passed and he might be feeling better, and when she returned, days later, still half-afraid, he'd gone, and she'd hardly seen him again. She learned afterwards that there'd been some sort of dreadful accident, but she never quite discovered what had happened, and he'd been in hospital for a long time. She'd tried to see him but they advised her not to. She didn't want to think of that time for it always upset her, even now. She thought he would come back when he was better, that he would try to see Chloe, or perhaps even take the girl away from her, for they'd been so fond of each other that she'd felt quite jealous. He sent money, and they'd been in touch through lawyers, that was all. Defiantly, she thought at first she'd be better off without his criticism, his anger, but now, oh, it was so difficult to manage, to make ends meet, even in this place, and there was hardly any time to enjoy herself, to have some fun. Most of the men she knew now just wanted to take advantage of her. There was no one to love her, to make her feel like a woman again.

Hurriedly she gathered up her handbag, her gloves, her key, from where they were lying, all over the flat, arranged a little grey jacket and scarf about her shoulders and neck, so that her soft hair was a fire-cloud above embers, or she was a phoenix, rising from ashes, and her eyes were wide and sad with the experience of grief and pain and loss. She opened the door, went out into the narrow hallway: there was the usual faint smell of something that she didn't like to think about, the usual untidy heap of brown envelopes and unopened circulars offering glorious prizes - dreams and bills, bills and dreams - and all the shabby squalor was too much for her. She stopped still there, leaning her forehead against the wall, and sobbed.

"Alan, oh Alan!" she whispered to the stains. Nothing had gone right for her since he left, nothing. "Alan, I can't manage on my own any more! I want us to be together again! But we'll do everything differently this time! I love you so much..."

She stepped into the yard, almost tripping over, her tall heels swaying from side to side like boats in a wind. The paving stones were cracked and broken, a web of weed-filled lines ran here and there - she'd seen a rat here once. The red sun was high and small in the sky, but the shoddy street was too far below, the leaning fences and the broken gates; old food wrappings blew in the gutters. The whole area seemed to be moving, rocking, unstable, as if a gust of wind might lift it altogether and cast it away in fragments of dust. Cold sunshine lit her face heartlessly, etched lines here and there, stripped the colour, scraped away the sweet bloom, as if in that moment the transition from youth to age were complete. The sharp light hurt her eyes, so that she had to raise one hand to shield them and for a while she could hardly see in all the brightness.

She felt she couldn't bear the onset of another spring, with all its brilliance, its hard, cold hope - but there were workmen in the road nearby, and one whistled and called out to her, something appreciative, though she didn't quite catch the words; it cheered her a little and she smiled at them, happy to be admired again. She caught a glimpse of herself in the tiny side mirror of a parked car, though she could hardly recognise herself there. She adjusted her hair quickly, an involuntary gesture.

She thought there could just be time after all to walk the longer way to the bus-stop, through the quiet leafy suburb that was next to her own, in that strange split-natured way of London. One day soon they might be able to move in somewhere there, perhaps, all of them together again; they were expensive houses, she knew, but she'd heard Alan was doing well now, earning more, had been promoted in his firm.

They would visit her father again together. Alan would get all the things that he needed. "Oh, Alan," she whispered again, and the soft heat of love for him swept through her as she thought of his voice, his hands, his eyes, the way he looked at her. "I've always loved you, Alan, truly, you didn't understand..."

Next door the little cat was crouched deep in the long grass, its body stretched and flattened to the ground, trembling, a small flame about to leap. Its tail flickered and twitched from side to side; every few minutes a tremor crossed its face, and its mouth opened to give some quick sound of excitement and anticipation of its catch, its red tongue curled. Evie wondered what it was the cat watched now, waiting, then pouncing. She frowned, she didn't like to think of the unpleasantness. Nature was very cruel, she thought again.

On the phone she'd worried for a moment at Alan's hesitancy, and she realised he might be unwilling at first to admit that he'd been wrong, that he still wanted her; that he might still be angry...

...but when he saw her, in the red, revealing dress, with the silken sound it made as she moved, when they were together again and she put her arms about his neck, drew his face down towards her own, and, oh, when she put her lips to his mouth, and her tongue found his...

Definition

The press and all the visitors have gone now, the doors are finally closed; but he lingers this last evening, looking away from the castle and its galleries towards the market-place, the city hall. It was his first exhibition here, in his home town, and almost the first time he has been back - and it was a success. His work was praised for its forward-looking techniques, its muted colours, its subtle variation of form and outline. His local connections were proudly noted. But now, looking back, almost thirty years back, Luke thinks of those connections again, of his school days, his family, how he would come up here to escape for a while, how it all started in this place...

"He's coming... he's here... *now, give it him!...*"

They'd got him. Up against the wall, after school. And they gave it him. The shock of their aggression and hatred was greater than the shock of pain through his body, and it remained with him for longer.

The lads in his class, half-boys, half-men, with their bunched fists and their sneering faces that were like fists, proving to him and to each other that they were normal, there was nothing wrong with them. The looks, the laughs he was used to already. The gestures, not quite hidden, glimpsed from the corner of his eye, stopping just as he turned. The ballet shoes sketched in delicate white on the blackboard; the words, hissed under the breath or shouted out - he hadn't realised there were so many. He could fight with his fists if he had to, his dad had seen to that, though Luke hated that way, the point-lessness of it, and there'd be other times, he knew, after school or in town, there'd be other people. But there was no way to fight the laughs, the gestures, the sneers.

There was nothing to fight when he was with Jon.

That was what he'd thought. Till yesterday.

"You decide then, Luke old son! But you'd best clear out of here if you can't behave like someone half-normal.

I'll not have it in this house..."

His dad *knew* now about Jon. His mum must have told him. And the bitter anger in the words hurt more sharply than the accustomed leathery swipe at the side of his head.

His mother still held a dishcloth and mug between her fingers as she followed him to the door, as if without them she had no function. She was always behind her husband or her son, always following one or the other; she walked with her head slightly bowed, a small animal burrowing in earth. Luke could almost see the division at the centre of her, like the line in the white roots of her hair before the crude bright brown began on either side. Her feelings for them both struggled with her need to shield one from the other; her wish to keep them apart fought with her need somehow to reconcile them, to bring them together. But she would always explain or excuse her husband.

"He will come round, love, or... perhaps you'll change your mind about things, Luke love, you'll grow out of it, maybe when you've left school, when you're older... People change..." She was so small, his mum, as if she'd been squeezed between the narrow terraced

39

houses or crushed by the weight of his dad's resentments, defined and diminished by *his* needs.

Luke stood with her at the doorstep, impatient for the fresh air outside. He hated the poky home that smelled of his father's constant smoking, his mother's desperation. He hated the ugly, ash-strewn furniture that had been there ever since he could remember and bore the shapes of his mum and dad; the TV always on in a corner of the living room, showing life on another planet closer to the sun, brightly-coloured, a land of smiles. The day that he might leave for ever could not come too soon either for himself or his dad, they were at one on that. Another year.

"He's had a rough life," his mum would say. She would stand at the window, dishcloth in hand, looking out as if she saw the years passing before her along the street. "His accident, and the mine closing, then everything shutting down... that Mrs Thatcher... He's had it hard, they've all had it hard here, the men. He doesn't mean it, really he doesn't, Luke love."

He wondered what she saw from the window of the passing of her own life.

But he knew that was the truth. To his dad, he

wasn't hard, as men had to be; he wasn't a *man*. And his father did mean it. Especially now. Luke was beginning to understand his father - disturbed and noisy, not so different from the boys at his school, but formed by the accidents and failures of his life and the ones that had happened all around him. He'd been a Union man, but now he was unemployed and disabled, left behind by time and change, everything that had defined him lost, disappeared. He didn't see Luke bringing hope for the future - whatever he saw from his own window, his son had no place there.

"They're victims," he'd said to Jon, yesterday. "Sad. Trapped. Only *he* doesn't know it." They were in Jon's room, overlooking the trees and late flowers of the comfortable back garden: a different type of house to his own, a different type of family.

He thought his mum should have stood up for him more, not 'Yes, yes Jack', and 'Let's have a cup of tea, love', not let his dad rant and shout. He pitied them both but as he turned at the gate to look back at the narrow, garden-less house, he saw through the window, sharp, like a cameo of married love, that his parents were embracing, his face on her shoulder, her cheek to his forehead. Her arms were around her husband as if he were her child.

He came here sometimes, to the castle and the galleries, to escape, and to think. From the well-kept gardens outside he could look on one side towards the town as if seeing himself still there, but far away and insignificant - finding perspective, the large become small, the present already the past. On the other side he could see the railway lines far below as they branched away to open country, different landscapes. It was late autumn now, the world in bronze, he thought, the trees like old men shedding their wealth before departing on their last journey; he could understand that sense of preparation and departure, of changing, of turning away... Inside the tall galleries it was quiet, except for the small animal sounds his trainers made on the wooden floor, the murmurs of other visitors, distant doors closing and opening, sounds emphasising space. Amongst the paintings and sculpture, the occasional displays, there was a different kind of perspective, a sense of history, and he could lose himself, but at the same time feel at home amongst the eloquent objects, open to their meanings.

This month there was an exhibition of pottery. He didn't know much about the pieces or their maker, but he liked the cool elegance, the pastel colours and elaborate shapes. They seemed to belong to a distant world, civilised, ritualised. He imagined the calm and order they might bring into everyday life - he thought of his own home, the smeared mugs and the dishcloths and the shouting.

At the entrance to each room he stopped to read the information boards, consciously prolonging his visit. Beneath a gilt-framed portrait of a bewigged eighteenth-century gentleman, he found bare biographical details:

Josiah Wedgwood was the youngest of twelve children born to a Staffordshire potter, who died when Josiah was eight, leaving his family in financial difficulties. Josiah was apprenticed in the same trade at the age of fourteen to his older brother. He contracted smallpox as a boy, which weakened one of his legs, so that it became difficult for him to work the wheel. But this weakness taught him to consider other, wider aspects of the craft...

They'd been to Stoke a few years ago for a football match, him and his dad - before things changed. It had been a good day: father and son, in a world that his father understood, where he felt at home. But Luke could still remember the run-down sadness of the town, charity shops along the main street, boarded-up windows, the heavy smell of burgers and chips. He wondered now how that might compare with the smoky Stoke of the old Potteries, the foggy dark of the streets. There were black and white photographs in the exhibition here showing how it once was, captions describing the enclosed heat of the kilns, the dust and the danger, all the gloom and hardship that had produced these pieces.

At that time, pottery was a small domestic industry producing basic items for work or home. But Wedgwood was not only a craftsman, he became a scientist and inventor also, and in due course a successful businessman, in this country and abroad.

Luke wondered how he'd done it. How did he leave all that behind him - crippling illness, the debt-ridden family, a failing industry, all those things that should have defined and limited him. How did he become so successful, so famous?

"Let's get out," he'd murmured to Jon as they lay together quietly. "We'll do what my dad wants. Soon. Next year, when we've finished here. Together." With his fingertips he touched Jon's raven's-wing hair, traced his profile, straight and fine like a carving, a cameo on pottery. Jon had a widowed mother and several older sisters, all successful, in the professions, in business. He wondered if they *knew*. Jon was clever, he was going to university, he was good at football. He fitted in. No-one messed with him or shouted after him.

In this first gallery were the teapots, jugs and coffee cans, the best-known pieces, with all their varied shapes, their pure soft colours – milk-white and blue, like Jon's skin, the white of his inner arm, that was sweeter and softer than his own mother's; his blue eyes, the grey-blue veins at his wrists.

This exhibition focuses on items made of jasper ware, a material that he developed and refined through years of experimentation, and which was perhaps his greatest achievement.

Luke glimpsed himself in the glass of a cabinet as he passed it, and studied what he saw impartially, as if it was a figure sculpted on a vase. A small figure; smooth, short gold hair revealing the shape of his head, which seemed slightly too big for his body, like a child's - a neat appearance, dark jeans and jacket. Behind him, the black-clad attendant was slumped on his chair in the corner of the gallery, his limbs stuck out at awkward angles, a broken puppet abandoned by his owners. Luke sensed that the man was staring at him, bored but sharp, appraising. He felt it in the small of his back, as he felt it at school, conscious of every glance; he felt that he too was an exhibit in a gallery, for all to walk around and comment upon.

In the next rooms were single, occasional items: medallions showing the events and the people of the time; physicians and scientists, explorers, statesmen, philosophers; an anti-slavery cameo of a kneeling

African in chains, and the words 'Am I Not a Man and a Brother?'.

Wedgwood was active in the Anti-Slavery movement and supported many humanitarian causes...

Luke remembered his dad shouting, red-faced, his head like a bullet, hard and smooth and lethal, his neck thrust forward. His own time as a Brother was long forgotten. "I don't care what the effing law says! I'm telling you, Luke, that lover-boy of yours, if I ever see him round here..." He was spitting his anger, hitting out with his walking stick towards his son's legs. Behind him, to one side, as always, his mother placed a hand on her husband's arm. "There's words for your sort!" he muttered, more quietly, turning away.

It was something new from his father, a new way to inflict hurt. And it had disturbed him.

"Whatever my dad says, there's still no real word for us, is there?" he'd said to Jon; and he wondered about other things for which there were no words. "*Homosexual* sounds like a disease, some sort of...

condition. We're not... we're not *gay*, are we? It's not how I feel. It's not a... a description... We're not *queer*... we're just... normal... just like everyone else is normal..." He remembered the words the boys in his class had yelled at him, and he saw how words are changed and bent, how there are meanings and there are words, and they are not the same. He saw how people make definitions for themselves and for other people.

Jon was silent. "We'll make our own words," Luke added. "Here's mine," he murmured slowly, turning towards Jon, leaning into him, making meaning: "Love you, live with you, follow you. Wherever. Whatever. But the words don't matter..."

Outside Jon's window the trees cast down a few bronze coins. They were alone in the quiet house.

Jon accepted his kiss, as he accepted his love, with cool, quiet grace, as if it was no more than his due; his beautiful profile was cameo-clear. Then he sat up, drew away. "Look, steady on Luke. I'm going to get married one day," he said. "Wife, kids, career: politics, or law. Management. Something clear and definite that I can aim for. I want to know where I am, where

I'm going. I'm not going to get caught out. Always hiding stuff. Like that politician, have the hacks after me all the time, hang their... their labels round my neck."

Luke was astonished, and shocked. He felt as if he'd smashed through glass, thinking it was an opening, and his face was gashed and bleeding amidst the splintered fragments. In the few weeks they'd been together, this was their first real conversation. And he was hurt: he saw that Jon took his love lightly, as he took everything, perhaps; he wondered what the word meant to him.

"But... there's no need to hide things! It's not illegal now, like it was before, not really... it's beginning to change, what the law says... It's only some people haven't caught up yet, like my dad, still stuck in the past..." His words stumbled out of him, less fluent than his feeling.

"And the rest of the class...?' Jon said. "There's always the rest of the class. The ones who never catch up. The ones who call you names. The ones who take their hang-ups out on you, feel tougher if they can make you sweat... making a reputation for themselves."

"But... they don't bother you, Jon. Not like they do me..."

"Who says they don't bother me?" Jon was angry, his blue eyes very dark. He stood, turning his back on Luke, looking towards the window.

"And what are you going to do then, what are your plans?" he asked more calmly, after a long silence, feeling perhaps that he had gone too far. He glanced at Luke. "When we leave here. What are your ambitions, Luke? You've never said..."

Jasper never became the easiest of bodies to work with or fire and there were still occasional obstacles to be overcome...

His father's anger, cruel and bitter, their constant fighting; the jeers and aggression of the boys at school; his love for Jon, and its rejection - these things were real, they were his life, they were what he was, he couldn't change them or deny them. But they were not all that he was or would be, they would not limit him. He would study, and work, and travel, there would be different places, different people...

He walked slowly through the galleries again, out-stared the attendant, then turned on his heel. From its frame, the 18th century face seemed to regard him thoughtfully as he left the room.

Outside, from the terrace, he looked down again to where, far below him, the railway spread its tracks across the countryside, fingers pointing to new places where ideas might be explored, plans made and remade; places without lines or limits, open and undefined.

As he walked back through the gardens, leaves drifted about his head as if they were his hopes and dreams released. He watched them turning and spinning, settling for a while, then he stooped and tossed them up and watched them fly once more.

Snow-Woman

She walked in the park most days, with Alfie and Topaz, though Topaz was very lame now. She liked to see the families here, all together, the children out from school for the winter holiday. The snow seemed to bring everyone closer, teenagers tobogganing, children making snowmen or snowballs to throw, or just tumbling and jumping into all the softness. And the little ones, the toddlers, always so delighted to find themselves walking and running at last, upright and exploring the world! She watched them especially, thinking of those times with Caroline – a long while ago, but fresh in her mind even now.

The snow came late this year, not till New Year's Eve, when it fell heavily, the clouds emptied inside out all at once. It stretched bright and smooth around them, as if the park had been iced like the Christmas cake she had at home, but with rainbow colours where the sunshine touched it. Then it could be almost too bright, and she had to close her eyes for a while.

Rachel could remember when they were one of the families enjoying their own small Christmas-times together here, not thinking about it coming to an end because, after all, families don't think of endings. On days like these, she could think that Caroline was still here with them, looking about her, knitting her brows earnestly as an adult, then smiling up at her mother, a little girl again; or throwing snow high into the air to see it shine against the sun. If she closed her eyes she could even imagine Caroline's children here too one day, somewhere around her, the generations continuing - slipping and falling as toddlers, sitting up again as youngsters, then running out from the trees, almost grown up! The first child and all the different ones, held together in some magic way by the snow.

At home again she gave the dogs their meal, and made some tea for herself. Bob would not be back till after six, another hour at least. Time goes more slowly in winter, she thought. There was still a yard or so of the Christmas cake left, with its forlorn decorations. She had made too much, as she always did, more than they would be able to eat, now that the guests had gone; its icy wastes glared up at her, and she closed her eyes again for a while.

She thought how they'd made the cake together for the first time that year, when Caroline was just on five, pale with her anxiety to learn, her pretty dark hair making her face seem even paler. She stood on a stool pulled up to the kitchen table to do the mixing, with one of Rachel's old aprons wrapped round her and reaching almost to her ankles.

"Now you must make a wish, Caroline," she said, "to mix in with the cake."

"You mustn't tell it to anyone," she added, her finger to her lips, but at last the child was almost bursting. Rachel put her arms tight round her, and listened to the whispered wish.

"Will you make one too, Mummy, to mix in?" Caroline asked after a few moments. There was a dusting of white flour, from the sieving, on her cheek. And Rachel stirred in her wish, with a fine show of mystery and magic.

And she knew that every year afterwards it would be the same, because every family has its small customs and ceremonies, reminding them of the things that are important.

Rachel had loved the snow when she was a child herself, for the silence it brought in a noisy street, the way the light was altered, and the sense that some great change had taken place in the small, everyday world she knew. And the sense that other changes, almost anything that she might dream of or imagine, could be possible while the snow lasted. Much later, Bob had proposed to her in the snow. He'd slipped, catching at her hands to save himself, on his knees, laughing; then suddenly serious, looking up at her. And years later, after Caroline was born and they brought her home from the hospital at last, she remembered how it was piled at the doorstep and the window-ledges, a perfect Christmas-card scene to greet them.

But it was different now, as if she'd come round the corner and found a familiar view quite altered. Time plays tricks with us sometimes, she thought, it is like a walking stick that folds or stretches out.

They'd waited seven years for a child; then one evening they walked from the doctor's surgery hand-in-hand, like children themselves again, knowing that the waiting was almost over - though the months till the birth seemed longer than the years that had passed. Caroline was born several weeks early, and two more difficult months went by before they could take her home. At first she appeared too frail and small to live, and Rachel knew that if something were to happen, after so long, she would not be able to endure it.

Caroline was fair when she was born, a little candle, lighting all the places in Rachel's life. As she grew older her hair became darker, her eyes grey as candle-smoke. She was solemn and funny by turn, happy to play by herself, then reaching up all at once to take her mother's hand and lead her towards some treasure she had found. Rachel felt that after the difficult years she was new-born herself, that she was growing and changing with her child. She had not known that she could be so happy.

She did not sleep well at first, always concerned for her baby, like any new mother, and she would listen to the quiet breathing in the cot beside her, in the darkness like a captive moth fluttering. She heard Bob on her other side, louder, with an occasional jerky snore, not moth-like at all.

She left the curtains open sometimes so that Caroline could see the moon outside if she woke, and she watched it herself as it crossed the narrow stretch of sky at their window, sometimes snagged with branches or smoky drifts of cloud, until it slipped away from sight, long before the morning.

She was thirty-three when the baby was born, and she did not have another. But all she wanted was to look after Caroline, to make up for the months of illness and pain. She promised her child that she would protect her from further harm, that she would grow up strong and safe.

And the images were always clear in her mind, though sometimes the details slipped away with the years, or a new recollection would emerge, and she realised that memory can sometimes confuse or fail. She thought how Caroline had loved the window-seat that looked out to the garden, whatever the weather. She would sit reading to herself, and she made up her own stories too, that were more real to her than the everyday things that happened; Rachel had been the same. Later, she would do her home-work sitting quietly in the sunlight there, schoolbooks scattered round, her thin legs tucked beneath her, white knees like knuckle-bones under the navy school skirt. Rachel hated to see her in the dark ugly things, her child in uniform, but Caroline loved to wear them. By then, Rachel remembered, she had more confidence, more colour.

There were several ways to walk, if there was time after the park, and she would ring the changes with the dogs, according to the time of day, or the weather. If it was fine she might take the short cut through the housing estate, then return home by the church. The whole neighbourhood had become shabby over the years since she and Bob first moved there, when Caroline was born, as if their married life had started only then. They'd spoken of moving since, but she always found reasons to stay. Her small routines resembled the faded wallpaper in the hall of their house, part of the fabric, holding things together. She would put on her old coat with the wavy hem, as it was the warmest, and the woolly hat that she'd had so long she'd forgotten where it came from. Their well-worn jackets and scarves hung there on the hall-stand, with an assortment of hats and bags and umbrellas; they looked to her like neighbours huddled together by a gate.

She needed to walk at this holiday time, as much as the dogs. During the day, the house was empty and quiet. Bob had returned to work already, but she still had a week to wait. She would put the radio on, or the television, but it was not enough. Nothing moved in the house unless she moved it, there was hardly a sound unless she made it. Nothing is as quiet as a house where there was once a child's voice.

"Daddy, do you know what is French for squirrel? Will you look at my drawings for tomorrow, please, Mummy? There's one of you." She had always loved drawing. The picture was small, with wild, frizzy hair, and Rachel wondered if that was indeed the way she appeared to her daughter. Later, Rachel recalled that the questions became harder: "What's Madagascar famous for, Dad?" or "When was the Industrial Revolution? Where did it start?" And sometimes she was making up the questions,

they became more impossible and far-fetched, and at last Rachel would realise and they would both smile. "What's the speed of light, Mum? How far to Mars!" Caroline had that husky uneven laugh, like a teenage boy's, so that Rachel felt she had to turn to see who else might be in the room.

The things they didn't know they looked up together, at first, in the big encyclopaedia which Bob had bought for her after she started school.

It was different later; they bought a computer, and Caroline looked things up by herself. Rachel learned how to use it too, the child became the teacher, and Rachel her child.

"Oh, really, Mum, what have you done *here? I just showed* you *..."*

When she was fifteen – Rachel smiled as she thought of it – Caroline told them that she wanted to be called Caz.

"Caroline - it's old-fashioned, Mum, like 1700 or something!" she said, with that mixture of affection and impatience coming to her face again. "Bonnets and para- sols, Mum!" she added, with her husky laugh. They all loved the costume dramas and watched them together, on

the old sofa, with Topaz and Alfie dozing at their feet.

"I think it's very pretty," Rachel ventured. She had always used the full name.

She tried her best with Caz, but her child would always be Caroline, whom she'd wanted for so long, and cared for more than anyone else.

And then, suddenly, Caroline – Caz – was turned eighteen, grown up at the speed of light.

"I think I'd like to travel for a bit," she told them quietly one morning, as they sat all together in the kitchen over a late breakfast, the sun slipping across from the window so that it found her, as it always did.

Rachel noticed how it striped her cheek and the old shirt she wore, and splashed her dark hair with gold and amber, almost unreal. It was these details that she thought about.

"Just for a few months, six or seven maybe, so I'll be back before you realise I've gone! Maybe India, or America" (and to Rachel it might have been Mars). "I've been planning it out with Lisa: we'll get jobs and work our way round. And then later, when we've got back, I'm going to try for art college, in London…" She'd been

unsettled for a while, uncertain what to do when she left school.

Rachel felt Bob's glance. She knew she must not let her silence last long, but the words would not come.

Caroline left that summer. Rachel knew she would be back quite soon – in all the years, what were a few months? – with her baggage, and her washing, and all her many boyfriends. But it wouldn't be the same, and she would be trying to stretch out the time that they had, knowing how quickly it would disappear, a snowflake in the sun.

When she walked through the estate, she would smile at the young mothers with their prams, and some of them let her admire their babies.

One afternoon she passed a yard where sometimes she'd seen a young girl - too young to be a mother, it seemed to her - and her young daughter, very pretty and pale, who made her think of Caroline. There was no sign of them today, but they'd made a snowman there, or perhaps it was a snow-woman, as she had a funny old hat with feathers on top, and there was a broken umbrella stuck under her arm, inside out.

She had a silly lopsided smile on her face, made of buttons. She looked sad and forlorn, ridiculous but brave, standing there alone in the cold and the fading light, as if she did not know she would melt one day, her umbrella quite useless against the elements. At first Rachel smiled, but then she stood and looked at the snow-woman for a long time, while the dogs grew annoyed, snuffling round her feet and nudging her legs, looking up at her, and she hardly noticed how late it was growing.

She liked to return home by the churchyard; it was pretty now in the snow, as the street lights were lit. Inside the church there was a scent of flowers, and the presence of others like her, who came to remember. And outside was the little cross, with the name upon it, half covered by snow:

Caroline Rose
4 years, three months

...and the few words beneath. And the date, yes, ten years ago... or was it ten weeks, ten days? The numbers had no meaning for her. "Time plays tricks with us," she thought again, "it deceives us like the snow."

"Dear Bob... oh, it's late, you're cold..." The chilly roughness of his winter coat on her cheek at least was real, bringing back the present. She wondered if in every marriage there is one who is parent to the other. He'd done his best; but she saw how sometimes he'd been frozen away, enduring his own long winter.

"Shall we... see about that new place now, Rachel love... ?"

"But..."

Their words were a kind of code, each phrase a summary, a reminder of all their conversations, their years together.

"Yes, of course... Yes, Bob, we should, maybe soon..."

She walked in the park most days, with Alfie and Topaz, moving into another year. She was glad she had the dogs to care for still. Topaz was very slow, but she liked to walk, her back slightly slanting, her tail moving a little from side to side as she went, the best she could manage. Her eyes were beautiful and sad, just as they were when they took her from the Shelter. Alfie came later - he was young, and full of enthusiasm.

It was not so pretty now, just grey sky, white sun. She thought it was the worst of these days, that there was no colour, as if colour had not yet been invented, or had vanished, as from a dead land. The children would soon be back at school; there would be no families, just a few people walking their dogs, smiling at strangers. The snow was melting, beginning in the open places; there were snowdrops, left behind as it retreated, their heads folded and bowed, as if remembering the past - but they too would soon be gone. Water dripped from leaves, slowly at first, then more quickly. Fragments of ice crumbled at the edges of the pond. The snow changes more as it retreats than when it first comes, she thought.

…perhaps she will visit us, when we are settled in our new place, and she will bring her friends, maybe her partner, and one day there will be a new baby, a grandchild…
She stayed till the light faded, the park about to close,

then she left the sheltered path by the trees where the burden of snow still lingered, turning away past the empty borders. The earth was loose and broken there and open to the clear, cold air.

A Quoi Bon Dire

Most Sundays it is the same. They invite her for lunch, the old lady, though it is a trouble to call for her, take her home again, down the long country lane at the end of the village. She still lives in the little lopsided cottage on the farthest corner, half-slipped into its own wild garden.

But she is alone now. Her husband passed away long years ago, no-one is sure quite how many years. Some of the people nearby can just remember him – tall and fine-looking, they say.

The village has changed a great deal since those days – though at the far edges, where the cottages are tumbled together and more overgrown, and the lanes wander into the fields, it is probably still the same as it has ever been.

It is Barry's turn to fetch her this Sunday, while Mum is at home cooking for all the family. His girl Sian, with her blue eyes and soft honey skin, is with him. It is special today – they have just become engaged. He is bringing Sian for lunch, and calling for the old lady as well. 'Two birds,' he says.

It is August; the air is blue and gold and glows as they do. They climb out of Barry's rusty car and walk down the path to ring the bell, waiting on the door-step to hear the old lady's slow faint tread. She always takes a while. They wonder what she can be doing; she knew when to expect them.

"She's just finishing the chapter."

"She's lost her keys. They're not where she put them last night!"

"The cat! Where's the cat!"

"She's checking the kettle's turned off."

"And all the taps! And..."

"Love you Sian," he says as they wait, and the sun shines on her upturned face; he touches it with his fingertips, tracing the patches of light there. "Always.

Even when you're an old lady like this one," and he smiles and gestures towards the cottage door, which is so overgrown he wonders how it might ever open again. Sian reaches up to run her hand through his hair: it is corn-brown, very fine, streaked gold now in the sun, and he wears it long, so that it touches his shoulders.

He has a habit of shaking his head back, freeing the hair from his face. She does it for him this time, makes it fan through her hands.

"Only ever you since I was six," she murmurs. "Guinness Book of Records," and they hold a long close kiss in the sunshine, forgetting.

They spring apart a little awkwardly when the door opens, though he is half-smiling still. "Sorry," he mutters to no-one in particular, his face bright.

After lunch she is quiet, the old lady. Sometimes she sleeps, in her chair in the corner. But Barry notices that later, with her cup of tea untouched before her, she is awake again, though her eyes are very far away, faded, cloudy and grey with all the memories, he thinks. Then they are silver too, and there is a little spillage of silver on her cheeks. Her lips are working, though she does not speak; her old hands, a crumple of bone and wrinkle and grey vein, move on her lap, as if they remember something that they touched once, how soft and fine it was.

"What's the story, Mum?" Barry asks, after he has taken the old lady home again.

> Seventeen years ago you said
> Something that sounded like Good-bye;
> And everybody thinks that you are dead,
> But I.
>
> So I, as I grow stiff and cold
> To this and that say Good-bye too;
> And everybody sees that I am old
> But you.

And one fine morning in a sunny lane
Some boy and girl will meet and kiss and swear
That nobody can love their way again
While over there
You will have smiled, I shall have tossed your hair.

Charlotte Mew [1869-1928]

Author's Notes

Definition
The notes concerning the pottery exhibition mentioned in the story are based partly on 'Wedgwood - The Felix Joseph Collection of 18th Century Jasper' (Catalogue of an Exhibition at Nottingham Castle Museum and Art Gallery, n.d. 2006?)

A Quoi Bon Dire
I have always loved the poem this story is based on, even though it is so simple, almost trite. I think it is the last line, the future perfect tense, that throws everything into the air and makes the verse into something that includes not only past and present but also a perfectly predicted and endless future...

Acknowledgements

The Indus Seals was placed second in the Exeter Writers' Short Story Competition 2016 and is also available on their website.

Snow-Woman was published in *November Wedding*, Pewter Rose Press, 2010.

I would like to thank both those organisations for their permission to publish the pieces here. I must also thank my writing group colleagues, Andy, Angela, Gaynor and Paul, for all their suggestions and help while I was working on these pieces. Thanks above all to Matthew Pegg of Mantle Lane Press for his tactful and knowledgeable support throughout the publication process.

This publication was supported using public funding by the National Lottery through Arts Council England

Mantle Lane Press would like to acknowledge support from Writing West Midlands.

Mantle Lane Press is a subsidiary of Mantle Arts Limited, which receives financial support from North West Leicestershire District Council.

LOTTERY FUNDED | ARTS COUNCIL ENGLAND

Supported using public funding by
ARTS COUNCIL
ENGLAND